For Eva —LZK

For Maria, te quiero mucho —EC

ABOUT THIS BOOK
The art for this book was done with watercolor in the dead of a Michigan winter, when the flowers were all gone. It was a miracle if you think about it. This book was edited by Samantha Gentry and designed by Karina Granda. The production was supervised by Bernadette Flinn, and the production editor was Marisa Finkelstein. The text was set in Century Schoolbook Std, and the display type is Sofa Serif.

Little, Brown and Company
Hachette Book Group
1290 Avenue of the Americas, New York, NY 10104
Visit us at LBYR.com

First Edition: February 2023

Little, Brown and Company is a division of Hachette Book Group, Inc.
The Little, Brown name and logo are trademarks of Hachette Book Group, Inc.

The publisher is not responsible for websites (or their content) that are not owned by the publisher.

Library of Congress Cataloging-in-Publication Data
Names: Kemp, Laekan Zea, author. | Chavarri, Elisa, illustrator.
Title: A crown for Corina / written by Laekan Zea Kemp; illustrated by Elisa Chavarri.
Description: First edition. | New York : Little, Brown and Company, 2023. | Audience: Ages 4–8. | Summary: Corina's abuela helps her select flowers that mean something to Corina from the garden for her Mexican flower crown that she will wear on her birthday, and explains the symbolic meaning of a birthday crown.
Identifiers: LCCN 2021038992 | ISBN 9780759556843 (hardcover)
Subjects: LCSH: Mexican Americans—Social life and customs—Juvenile fiction. | Birthdays—Juvenile fiction. | Flowers—Symbolic aspects—Juvenile fiction. | Grandmothers—Juvenile fiction. | Grandparent and child—Juvenile fiction. | CYAC: Mexican Americans—Fiction. | Birthdays—Fiction. | Grandmothers—Fiction. | Flowers—Fiction
Classification: LCC PZ7.1.K463 Cr 2023 | DDC [E]—dc23
LC record available at https://lccn.loc.gov/2021038992

ISBN 978-0-7595-5684-3

PRINTED IN CHINA

APS

10 9 8 7 6 5 4 3 2 1

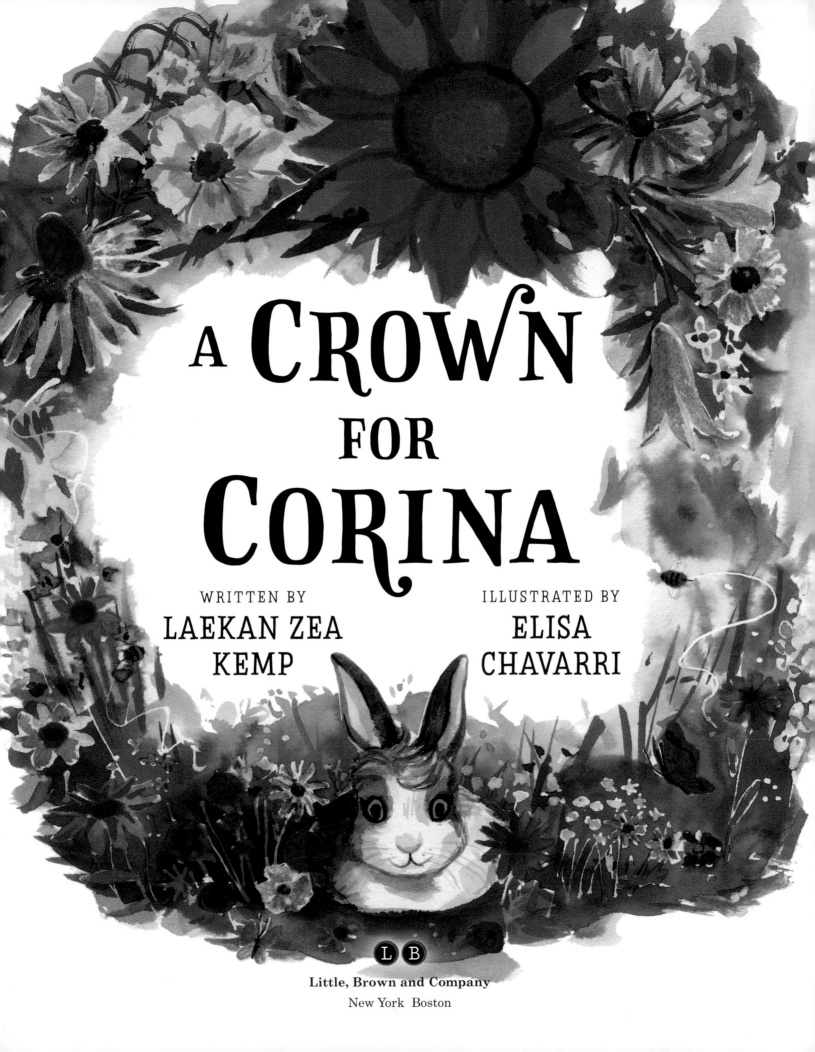

A CROWN FOR CORINA

WRITTEN BY
LAEKAN ZEA KEMP

ILLUSTRATED BY
ELISA CHAVARRI

Little, Brown and Company

New York Boston

Abuela's garden is bursting with colors so bright that it looks like la tierra is throwing una fiesta.

Today, the party is for me.

It's my birthday, which means I get the biggest corona with the most beautiful flowers picked from Abuela's garden.

Abuela hands me my canasta. "Make sure you save some of the roses for me."

I run through the flowers, feeling their petals graze
the tips of my fingers. Some are soft and smooth,
others prickly. Some even make me sneeze.

I reach the bluebonnets first and trace a finger down their bell-shaped petals.

Abuela kneels next to me. "Every flower in your crown must tell your story, Corina. Who you are and where you come from." She plucks a purple orchid from one of the clay pots.

"Your abuelo used to buy me orchids for our anniversary every year." She places it in her basket. "Wearing it in my crown reminds me that I am loved."

I look out at Abuela's garden, at the bees and
butterflies, and I see a language I never knew before.
One spoken not in words but in the prick of a cactus
needle, in the bright orange plumes of a bird of paradise,
and in the sweet scent of a chocolate cosmos.

"Now, tell me," Abuela says, "what do the bluebonnets mean to you?"

"The bushy white tips remind me of Fofo's tail. He loves hopping through the flowers almost as much as I do. He's family," I say.

"Of course he is," she says, smiling, "which means these conejos belong in your crown."

I pick a sunflower for Mamá because her favorite color is yellow, sword lilies for Papá to match our sword fights before bed, and morning glories for Abuelo because they look like the trumpet he used to play.

"And this one's for you." I hand Abuela a bushel of coneflowers. "It looks like your gardening hat."

"They're beautiful, mija." She places them in my canasta with the others.

"Now it's time to tell the next part of the story. Who you want to be," Abuela says.

"Is it like making a birthday wish and blowing out the candles?"

She nods. "Just like that."

I pluck bright yellow esperanzas because they
mean hope, daisies because they are strong enough
to grow anywhere, and mistflowers because their
sweet nectar is the butterflies' favorite.

As Abuela helps me fasten them all to my crown, I ask, "Why do we wear las coronas, Abuela?"

"When we place la corona on our head, we become its roots, reaching back through time to hold on to the things that matter. Our family. Our history."

I touch the flowers again, one by one, and I see it all.

MY STORY.
MAMÁ'S.
ABUELA'S.

As guests arrive for my party, I tell them the story of my crown, of all the ways that I am rooted in the people I love.

At night, I don't want to take it off.
Not even after Mamá makes me put on my pajamas.

Not even after Papá finishes my bedtime story.

A few petals fall onto the bed, some of the flowers beginning to droop.

Abuela comes to sit next to me. "Do you know why the flowers are beginning to wither, Corina?"

I shake my head.

She takes my hand. "Because we pulled them from the soil, and nothing can survive that far from home." She holds me close. "You'll have other coronas, Corina, but just one family. Remember that."

Through the window I can see Abuela's flowers
swaying in the moonlight. Each new bloom marks a new
season. The coronas keep time too. This one says I am
one year older. That I am Corina Casarez.

DAUGHTER.
GRANDDAUGHTER.
WISH MAKER.

I slip the crown off my head, but the love isn't gone. I still have my memories of the day I spent with Abuela in her garden, learning to speak the language of the flowers.

And I still have more springtimes, more birthdays, more chances for my dreams to bloom.